BBC CHILDREN'S BOOKS
Published by the Penguin Group
Penguin Books Ltd, 80 Strand, London WC2R 0RL, England
Penguin Putnam Inc., 375 Hudson Street, New York, New York 10014, USA
Penguin Books Australia Ltd, 250 Camberwell Road, Camberwell, Victoria 3124, Australia
Canada, India, New Zealand, South Africa
First published in 2002 by BBC Worldwide Limited.
This edition published by BBC Children's Books, 2005
10 9 8 7 6 5 4 3
Illustrations by Magic Island
Text, design and illustrations © BBC Children's Books, 2005
The Tweenies name, logo and characters are trademarks of the
British Broadcasting Corporation and are used under licence. © BBC 1998-2001
Tweenies is produced by Tell-Tale Productions for BBC Television
BBC and logo © and ™ BBC 1996. CBeebies and logo ™ BBC. © BBC 2002
All rights reserved.
ISBN 1 405 90092 X
Printed in Italy

That's My Picture!

One day, the Tweenies watched a video about animals.

"I'm going to paint a picture of my favourite animal," said Milo.

Judy put out the paint pots on the messy table and Milo got ready to paint his picture.

"I'm going to paint a picture of a cat," he said.

Milo dipped his brush in the paint and made a big circle for the cat's head. Then he added the eyes, ears and mouth, and left it to dry.

Bella came along.
"Oh, a rabbit!" she said. "That's my favourite animal. But it needs a body!"

"I know," she said. "I'll finish the picture!"
She picked up the paintbrush, dipped it in the
paint, and painted the body of the rabbit.
Bella left the painting to dry.

Later, Fizz walked past the messy table.
"Oh, look," she said. "A horse! That's my
favourite animal. But it needs legs!"

"I know," she said. "I'll finish the picture!"
She picked up the paintbrush, dipped it in the paint, and painted the legs of the horse.
Fizz went to read a book while the paint dried.

Then, along came Jake.
"Oh – a lovely picture of a zebra!
That's my favourite animal," said Jake. "But
needs stripes!"

"I know," he said. "I'll finish the picture!"
He picked up the brush, dipped it in
the paint, and carefully painted the
zebra's stripes.

Now all the Tweenies had painted part of the picture and everyone had their own idea about what animal it was.

As Max was walking past the messy table, he saw the picture.

"Oh, look at this. A lovely painting of a tiger," he said to himself. "But it needs whiskers and a tail!" Max picked up the paintbrush and quickly finished the picture of the tiger.

Then he made a label for it. Max was so pleased with the painting, he stuck it onto a piece of card, put it in a frame and hung it on the wall so everyone could see it.

TIGER

When the Tweenies saw the picture they were very surprised.

"Hey, who's been messing around with my cat?" asked Milo.

"That's not a cat, it's supposed to be a rabbit," said Bella.

"No, it's not – it's my horse!" said Fizz, crossly. "At least it was a horse, until someone changed it."

"No, no. It's not a horse, it's my zebra," insisted Jake.

Max realized what had happened and explained that everyone thought it was something different, but now it was a tiger.

"But it should have been my painting of a cat," said Milo sadly.

"Well, a tiger is a kind of cat," explained Max.

"Is it? I didn't know that," said Jake.

"Great – I've always wanted a pet cat. Can we get a tiger, then?" asked Milo.

The Tweenies all agreed it would be fantastic to have a pet tiger. They decided to sing a song about tigers.

I wish I had a tiger,
He'd make a lovely pet.
If I could have an animal,
A tiger I would get.

Oh I wish I had a tiger,
I'd love to hear him roar.
I'd teach him how to count,
One, two, three, FOUR!

Oh if I had a tiger,
I'd take him for a walk.
He'd growl at all my friends and
I'd teach him how to talk.

I wish I had a tiger,
I'd stroke his furry head.
And when it's time for sleeping,
I'd tuck him up in bed.

So can we have a tiger?
You know it would be fun!
A tiger in the playroom,
A friend for everyone!

Doodles came along and asked them what they were singing about.

"We were singing about a tiger," explained Bella.

"Yes, we want a pet tiger to come and live here with us," added Jake.

Doodles couldn't believe his ears.

"Everyone needs a pet to look after," Bella pointed out.

"But you've got a pet, right here," he woofed. "Don't you like me any more?"

"Oh, Doodles, of course we like you," said Fizz, stroking his fluffy red and yellow coat.

"We just thought it would be fun to have another pet," said Milo.

Max explained that tigers live in the jungle and not in houses.

"So, you see, everyone, we're really lucky to have Doodles. Tigers don't make very good pets."

"No, they don't," agreed Doodles.

"Doodles belongs here with us," said Max.

"And tigers belong in the jungle."

The Tweenies realised how lucky they were
to have a wonderful pet like shaggy, furry,
fluffy, cuddly Doodles.

THE END